*To my friends
Sara and Nicole Mallie, two excellent readers,
and to their parents, Ann and Wayne*

Series

The Biggest Bully in Brookdale
It's Not Fair
The Richest Kid in the World
Nobody's Friend
The Great Director
Skin Deep

Contents

Chapter 1	Tess's Lie	7
Chapter 2	Mrs. Munro's Surprise	16
Chapter 3	Tess in a Jam	26
Chapter 4	Tess Fesses Up	38
Chapter 5	The Kids Meet Aunt Claire	47

Tess's Lie

"**M**y mom won the big prize!" exclaimed Tess Munro, skipping down the sidewalk with The Tree House Kids. "*Fifty whole dollars!* The guy at the grand opening of Clausen's Department Store just pulled her name out of the big jar!"

"Wow!" said Ben. "That's great!"

"There must've been a *zillion* names in that jar!" Tess said, beaming. "But the guy pulled out the slip of paper with Mom's name on it!"

"What's your mom going to do with the money?" Roger asked.

"She can't decide," said Tess. "She has to spend it at Clausen's. But she said she'd get something for the whole family." She grinned. "I can't wait to tell the other kids.

Nobody in my family has ever won *anything!*"

"Neither has mine," Roger said.

"I won a pencil in preschool once," Ben said. "I was the quietest kid during story time. That was because I fell asleep."

Tess, Ben, and Roger were on their way to school. Tess and Ben were in third grade, and Roger was in second. They had been best friends since the first day of school, when Ben and Tess discovered a mean kid beating up Roger.

The three had started a club called The Tree House Kids. Nearly every day after school they'd met in a tree house in a neighbor's yard to talk about how they could stop the kid from bullying them. Ben, Tess, and Roger became good friends.

Their problem with the bully finally ended. But they'd loved playing in the tree house and decided to keep meeting as a club.

Tess couldn't stop smiling. This was an exciting day, and she was anxious to tell the other kids. It would be fun to see their faces when she told them about her mother's $50 prize!

When The Tree House Kids got to school, they found a large group of kids on the playground gathered around Julie Walters, a girl in their class.

"She's on TV and in the newspaper all the time!" Julie was saying. "Reporters just follow her around! They write down everything she says!"

The kids surrounding Julie all looked very excited. They said things like "Oooo!" and "Wow!" and "Fantastic!" all at the same time.

"What's going on?" Tess asked Sam Flagg, who was standing at the edge of the crowd of kids.

"Julie's grandmother is in the House of—of—what is it?"

"The House of Representatives," said Angie Clymer, who was standing next to him.

"Yeah," said Sam. "She was just elected. Now she gets to move to Washington, D.C.!"

"Yeah," said Britt Spector. "She's *famous!*"

Ben and Roger grinned, but Tess just said, "Oh."

Suddenly Tess didn't feel so proud of her

mother's $50 prize. The kids wouldn't be interested in hearing about that now. What was a measly $50 compared to having a famous grandmother who's on TV all the time?

"I wish *my* grandmother was famous!" Tam Ling said. She turned to Tess, her eyes wide with excitement. "Julie's so lucky!"

Tess frowned and stuck out her lower lip. She had been so excited to tell everyone about her mother's prize, and now her news was ruined.

"Don't you wish you had a famous grandmother?" Tam asked. "It would be so much fun to visit her!"

"That's not as great as my aunt," Tess murmured.

Tam Ling looked at Tess curiously. "Who is your aunt?" she asked.

"Aunt Claire," Tess said. "She lives in Los Angeles. She's a really great director."

"A director?" Tam said. She looked impressed. "You mean, like in the movies?" Tess saw that Tam Ling's face was changing. Now she looked more interested in hearing about Tess's Aunt Claire than about Julie's grandmother. That made Tess feel important.

The only trouble was that Aunt Claire had never directed a movie in her life. She had only directed plays in the community theater, where people who lived close by put on plays just for fun.

But Tess didn't want to tell that to Tam Ling. Tam looked so excited, because she thought that Aunt Claire was a famous movie director.

Several other kids turned to face Tess.

"Your aunt directs *movies?*" asked Britt Spector.

"Uh, yeah," said Tess.

She couldn't tell them the truth now! Besides, it felt so good to have their attention.

"What movies did she direct?" Britt asked.

Nobody was paying attention to Julie Walters now. They were all listening to Tess. Even Julie looked interested in hearing about Tess's aunt.

"She's directed lots of movies!" said Tess. "I even saw her on TV in the audience at the Academy Awards!"

"Wow!" A murmur of awe came from the crowd of kids.

Roger nudged Ben and spoke quietly. "I didn't know Tess's aunt was a famous director," he said.

"Neither did I," said Ben, frowning.

"Has she directed any big movie stars?" Kara LaMasters asked.

"The biggest!" said Tess, looking around her at all the excited faces.

"Who? Who?" all the kids wanted to know.

"Just name a famous movie star," Tess said. "Aunt Claire's worked with *all* of them!"

Tess felt like a movie star herself, surrounded by friends who were all asking her questions. It was so exciting!

"How come you never told us about her?" Sam asked.

"It never came up," Tess said, shrugging.

"Does she ever come to visit you?" asked Tam Ling.

"No, she's too busy," Tess said.

That was really true. Aunt Claire was a very busy person. She worked in a doctor's office all day and then spent a lot of her evenings at the theater. Tess could only re-member her aunt visiting once.

"I hope we can meet her sometime," Tam said. "I want to ask her about the stars she's worked with!"

"I don't think she'll visit anytime soon," Tess said.

Tess was very glad of that! She would sure be in a jam if Aunt Claire really *did* come to town!

The bell rang, and the kids started walking toward the school building.

Ben took hold of Tess's arm and pulled her away from the other kids. Roger followed.

"Tess, I didn't know your Aunt Claire was a famous director," Ben said.

Tess suddenly felt guilty. Ben was her best friend, and she had never told him a lie.

"Oh, didn't I tell you that?" she said. She tried to sound innocent, but her voice came out sounding kind of squeaky.

"Did you make it up?" Ben asked.

Tess looked at Ben's face. He didn't look mad. He just looked serious.

Roger didn't look mad either. He looked curious.

"Well," Tess said. "It started out the truth. Aunt Claire really *is* a great director."

"In the movies?" Roger asked.

"Well, no," Tess said slowly. "In the community theater." Then she quickly added, "But it's in Los Angeles, near Hollywood."

"That's not the same thing," Ben said.

Tess shrugged. "Okay, so I exaggerated a tiny bit."

"You exaggerated a whole lot!" Ben said.

"Actually, what you did was lie," Roger said. He blinked behind his big glasses.

"Well, so what?" Tess cried. "Julie was bragging to everybody about her stupid famous grandmother."

"But Julie was telling the truth," Ben pointed out.

"But I *started out* telling the truth!" Tess said, her voice getting louder and louder. "I just said Aunt Claire was a great director. I couldn't help it if Tam decided I was talking about the movies!"

"You could've told Tam that's not the kind of director you meant," Ben said.

"Oh, big deal!" Tess yelled. "So I told a fib."

"Quite a few," Roger offered.

"So what!" Tess cried. *"Who cares?"*

Ben shrugged. "Okay," he said. "I just hope the kids don't find out that your Aunt Claire isn't a famous director."

"How could they find out?" Tess's eyes narrowed. "Unless you guys tell them!"

"I won't tell," Ben promised.

"Me neither," Roger said.

"Good," Tess said. "Come on. We'd better not be late for school."

She turned and headed toward the school. Ben and Roger followed.

Tess was mad that the guys had made such a big deal about her little lies to the kids. It wasn't even her fault the whole thing happened!

Ben and Roger had better not say any more about it, Tess thought angrily as she pulled open the school door.

Besides, there was no harm done. The kids would never find out the truth.

2

Mrs. Munro's Surprise

Tess was the most popular student in the whole school that day. Their teacher, Ms. Conley, asked the third graders to form study groups in social studies. All the kids wanted Tess in their group.

"Be in my group!" Britt Spector said, waving her hand at Tess.

"Tess, be in *mine!*" called out Tam Ling.

"No way!" said Patrick Doyle. "Tess is my buddy. You'll be in my group, won't you, Tess?"

Tess turned to look from side to side as she heard voices calling out her name. She didn't know what to do. She liked all the kids in her class and didn't want to say no to anyone.

Ms. Conley made it easy for her. She assigned Tess to Tam Ling's group.

But Ms. Conley wasn't out on the playground at recess when 10 different kids asked her to play with them. And Ms. Conley wasn't in the cafeteria when kids at almost every table called her to eat with *them* today.

Tess had never felt so popular. It was a wonderful feeling.

Ben watched quietly when kids surrounded Tess on the playground. He didn't say a word in gym class when the captains of the soccer team argued over which team Tess would join.

He hardly even glanced at Tess when she left his lunch table to sit with other kids.

But Tess knew Ben was thinking about what was happening, and she felt guilty. Ben knew she was suddenly popular because of the lies she had told about her Aunt Claire.

So she tried not to look at Ben whenever the kids were around asking her about her famous aunt.

During the afternoon recess, Tess walked out of the school with Tam Ling, Angie Clymer, Kara LaMasters, and Britt Spector. Ben went to play with Sam Flagg and Patrick Doyle.

"I just keep thinking about your Aunt Claire," Tam Ling said.

"Me too," said Britt. "Have you ever visited her in L.A.?"

"Yeah," Tess said. "She has a nice home."

Tess thought of Aunt Claire's little home on a quiet street in Los Angeles.

"I bet she lives in a mansion!" Britt said.

"I've seen pictures of homes that the big stars have in L.A.," said Angie. "They're even bigger than Patrick's house." Angie was talking about Patrick Doyle's home, the largest house in town.

"What does your aunt's mansion look like?" Tam Ling asked Tess. "Does it have a swimming pool?"

"Sure," said Tess. "It's as big as the pools the Olympic swimmers use."

Britt pulled out a piece of paper from her pocket. "Can I have your aunt's address?" she asked.

Tess was startled. She stared at Britt.

"Aunt Claire's address?" she said. "Why do you want her address?"

Britt laughed. "I want to *write* to her, silly!"

"Ooo," said Tam, her eyes sparkling with excitement. "Good idea! Can I have the address too? I want to write and ask her about all of the stars she's worked with!"

Tess's heart began beating very hard. She couldn't let the girls write to Aunt Claire! Then Aunt Claire would know Tess had made up stories about her, and the girls would certainly learn the truth.

"But I don't have Aunt Claire's address!" Tess protested. Her palms were now wet, and her heart was beating faster.

Britt stared hard at Tess. "Are you *sure* your aunt is a famous Hollywood director?"

"Of *course!*" Tess cried. "Why? Don't you believe me?"

Britt continued to stare at Tess. "I think it's weird that you don't have your own aunt's address."

Tess tried to swallow. It felt as if there were a baseball stuck in her throat.

"I just don't have it *now*," she said.

19

"So when can you get it?" Britt demanded.

"I don't know."

"Well," Britt said, folding her arms in front of her, "I don't think I believe this whole story about your Aunt Claire."

"You don't have to!" Tess cried. She felt her face getting very hot. "I don't care if you believe me or not!"

But she did care. She cared very much. She didn't want her friends to think she had made up all those lies about her Aunt Claire.

She looked at the other girls. She couldn't tell whether or not they believed her.

"Come on, Tam," Britt said, nudging her friend. "Let's go see if Julie wants to play four-square."

Tam nodded and followed Britt down the slope on the playground.

Tess turned anxiously to Angie and Kara. "Want to play tetherball?"

There was a short pause before either of them answered.

"Sure," said Kara in a soft voice.

"Okay," said Angie.

They were going to play with her, but Tess could tell something had changed. Did they think she was lying too? She couldn't tell for sure.

After school, Tess found her mother's car waiting at the curb.

"Hi, honey," her mother said. "Get in. I have a surprise for you."

Her mother looked past Tess. "Oh, there's Kara and Angie. Think they might like a ride?"

Tess shrugged and got in the car.

"Kara! Angie!" Mrs. Munro called out. "Would you girls like a ride home?"

"Sure!" they said. They ran to the car and got in the back seat.

"Where are Ben and Roger?" Tess's mother asked. "It'll be a tight squeeze, but I don't want to leave them behind."

"Ben had a doctor's appointment," Tess said. "I haven't seen Roger."

Her mother started the car. "Okay, let's go then. I'll drop you girls off at home," she said, glancing in the rearview mirror at Kara and Angie. "Then, Tess, we're going to the airport."

"How come?"

"That's my surprise!" said Tess's mother.

"Aunt Claire is coming for a visit! Isn't that wonderful?"

Tess's mouth popped open. Kara and Angie squealed in the back seat. Mrs. Munro glanced in the rearview mirror, surprised at the girls' reaction.

Tess's heart was thundering in her ears. "But Aunt Claire is so busy—"

"I know!" said her mother. "But she decided on the spur of the moment to drop her work and take a little vacation."

"Oh, that's so exciting!" Kara exclaimed.

"Can we meet her?" asked Angie. "Can we ride along to the airport with you?"

Tess's heart nearly stopped. *No, no!* she pleaded silently with her mother. *Don't let them come!* Oh, this was awful! Just awful!

"I'd love to have you girls come with us," said Mrs. Munro, "but we haven't asked your parents' permission. Also, I'm afraid this little car would be uncomfortably crowded with Aunt Claire and all of her luggage."

There was a disappointed murmur from the back seat.

Mrs. Munro turned the car onto Angie's street. She looked into the rearview mirror again at Angie and Kara. "I'm a little surprised. Why the interest in Tess's aunt?"

"Are you kidding?" said Kara. "I've never met a director before!"

"I told them Aunt Claire was a great director," Tess said quickly. She was afraid the words *movie director* would come up next, so she changed the subject. "Aunt Claire can sleep in my bed. I'll sleep on the couch."

"Thanks, honey," her mother said. "I was just going to ask if you'd mind."

A minute later she stopped the car at the curb in front of Angie's house.

"Thanks for the ride, Mrs. Munro," Angie said.

"You're welcome," Tess's mother said. She turned around to look at Angie and Kara in the back seat. "Would you girls like to come over after school tomorrow and meet Aunt Claire?"

The girls squealed again. Angie said, "Oh, *can* we?" and Kara said, "We'd love to!" at the same time.

Mrs. Munro laughed. "Well, I'm glad you're so excited!"

"Could we invite a few other kids over?"

asked Kara. "Maybe Britt Spector and Tam Ling?"

"Sure," Mrs. Munro said. "The more the merrier!" She patted Tess's arm. "We'll have a good time with Aunt Claire."

Tess sank down into her seat as the girls got out of the car and said good-bye.

This was the worst thing she could imagine. All the kids would be coming over tomorrow, expecting to meet a famous movie director.

This was horrible. *Absolutely horrible!*

Tess in a Jam

Tess rode with her mother to the airport. Aunt Claire's plane arrived at four o'clock.

Aunt Claire ran to them from the boarding gate. She threw her arms around Tess's mother. Then she gave Tess a big hug. She told them how happy she was to be in Brookdale visiting them.

Tess was glad to see Aunt Claire. But she was feeling terrible about telling the lies. And it was even worse knowing the kids would find out about those lies tomorrow. Maybe they'd hate her and never want to play with her again.

Tess felt as if she had a rock in her stomach.

She smiled at Aunt Claire and answered the questions her aunt asked about school on the way home from the airport. But Tess was hardly thinking about what she was saying. She couldn't think of anything but how awful tomorrow was going to be.

Tess's 16-year-old sister Ashley was home from school when they arrived. Ashley visited with Aunt Claire for a while. Then she said she had homework to do.

Tess followed Ashley upstairs to their room.

"Can I talk to you, Ash?" she said, stopping in the doorway.

Ashley tossed her sweater onto her bed. "What do you want?" she said. "I have a math test tomorrow, and Brian said he'd call later. I don't have much time."

"Well—" The words weren't going to come easily. Tess stepped into the room. "Well, what if you told somebody something that wasn't exactly true?"

Ashley turned to face Tess. "A lie, you mean."

Tess scowled. "I guess."

"So you told somebody a big fat lie, right?" Ashley said, plopping down on the bed.

"Okay, so it was a lie," Tess said. She

came over and sat on the bed facing her sister. "I don't know how to get out of it."

"What did you lie about?" Ashley asked.

"Aunt Claire," Tess said. "I told my friends she was a famous movie director."

"Boy, was that stupid!" Ashley exclaimed. "Why would you tell them a lie about Aunt Claire when she was on her way here?"

"Because I didn't *know* she was on her way here!" Tess cried. "And now Mom invited my friends to come over and meet Aunt Claire tomorrow after school."

Ashley laughed. "You're kidding!"

"I'm not kidding, and it's not funny!" Tess said.

Ashley shook her head. "Boy, did you ever get yourself in trouble *this* time!"

"What should I do?" Tess said.

"I don't think there's anything you can do," said Ashley. "The kids'll come over tomorrow. They're sure to find out Aunt Claire isn't a famous movie director. Boy, I hate to think what they'll say about *that!*" She grinned. " 'Liar, liar, pants on fire.' "

"Well, thanks a whole lot," Tess said. "You really made me feel better!"

"You got yourself into this!" said Ashley, bouncing up off the bed. "Don't blame me!"

Ashley pulled out her desk chair and sat down. Her back was to Tess. Tess got up from the bed and walked out of the room. She sat down at the top of the stairs feeling miserable.

She could hear her mom's and Aunt Claire's faint voices downstairs. She leaned against the wall next to her.

What was she going to do? She felt as if she had gotten onto a train that was speeding out of control. Wasn't there any way to get off? What would happen tomorrow afternoon when her friends came over? Would her life be changed forever?

Just then, she thought of something and sat up. Mrs. Pilkington, who owned the tree house the kids used for their club, was very wise. Maybe *she* could help Tess get out of this mess!

That was it. If *anyone* could help her figure out what to do about her lies, it was Mrs. P.!

"Well, Tess, how nice to see you!" Mrs.

Pilkington said. She stood at her back door. She was wearing jeans, a sweatshirt, and sneakers. Beyond her, Tess could see her neatly kept kitchen. "Are The Tree House Kids meeting today?"

"No," Tess said. "But would you come up to the tree house with me?"

"Sure," said Mrs. P. "Let's go."

Tess and Mrs. Pilkington crossed the back yard. They climbed the fence at the side of her garage, climbed onto the garage roof, and stepped into the tree house.

Tess looked out over Mrs. P.'s yard. She could see the rooftops of houses a whole block away.

"I love this tree house," Tess said.

"So do I," said Mrs. Pilkington, standing next to her.

"Sometimes I wish I could just stay up here," Tess said. "I wouldn't have to go to school. I wouldn't have to see anybody."

"This is a good place to get away for awhile," agreed Mrs. P. "But then it's always good to go home again."

Tess thought about going home again. That made her think of Aunt Claire's visit, and Tess's stomach turned a somersault.

"I wish I didn't have to go home for a whole year!" Tess said.

"Tess," Mrs. P. said gently. "Would you like to sit down and talk for awhile?"

Tess was glad Mrs. Pilkington suggested it. She sat on the floor of the tree house and leaned against the wall. Mrs. P. sat cross-legged next to her.

"You sound a little unhappy today, Tess," Mrs. P. said.

"You said it!" Tess said. "Mrs. P., I don't know how I get myself into these messes."

"What messes?" Mrs. P. asked.

Tess explained about making up the story about Aunt Claire. She told Mrs. P. how all the kids wanted to meet her aunt, and now her aunt was here!

"And they're all coming over tomorrow after school," Tess said. "They're going to ask my aunt about all the movie stars she knows. And then I'm *really* going to be in trouble!"

Mrs. P. nodded thoughtfully. "Yes, I guess that is a bit of a mess," she said.

"It's a *humongo* mess!" Tess cried. "I don't know why I started saying all those things! I was so stupid!"

"Well, I think I understand how that could happen," said Mrs. P. "I'll bet it felt pretty great when all the kids wanted to hear about your aunt."

Tess gazed up into the trees and remembered. "It was *wonderful*," she said.

"Everybody likes to feel important," Mrs. P. agreed.

Tess looked back at Mrs. Pilkington. "But now everything's so awful! I know I did a really bad thing. I know I shouldn't tell lies."

"Well, lying does make problems," agreed Mrs. P.

"I bet Ben thinks I'm horrible," Tess said. "He didn't say much, though. He didn't tell any of the kids I wasn't telling the truth."

"Ben is a very good friend," said Mrs. Pilkington. "And I'm sure he doesn't think you're horrible. He's your friend, and he loves you no matter what."

Tess didn't know whether or not Ben really *loved* her, but it was good to hear Mrs. Pilkington say he might.

"Do *you* think I'm horrible, Mrs. P.?" Tess asked.

"Of course not!" Mrs. P. said, smiling. "You're my friend, Tess. I'm sorry that you're in a jam, but I love you, too, no matter what."

Tess smiled in spite of herself. "Thanks, Mrs. P."

"And God loves you, too, you know," Mrs. Pilkington said. "I think this might be a problem you should turn over to Him."

Tess was surprised. "But I did a bad thing!" she said. "Doesn't God punish us for doing bad things?"

"No," said Mrs. P. "God loves us so much, He sent Jesus to take the punishment for the bad things we do. Are you sorry for telling those lies?" asked Mrs. P.

"Are you kidding?" said Tess. "I wish I could go back to this morning and start the whole day over again! I'd keep my big, stupid mouth shut this time!"

"All you have to do is tell God that you're sorry."

"That's all?" Tess asked.

Mrs. P. nodded. "Then ask God to forgive you, and ask Him to help you with this problem."

Tess suddenly felt hopeful. "Do you think God might give my friends the chicken pox or something so they can't come to school tomorrow?"

Mrs. P. smiled. "No, I don't think so," she said. "But wait and see what happens. I think God will help you know what to do."

"I'm still going to get in trouble, right?" asked Tess.

"Maybe," said Mrs. P. "But I'm sure it'll be something you can handle."

"I'm scared," Tess said.

"I know," said Mrs. P. "But you don't need to be scared. Just put your trust in God. Thank Him for forgiving you, and then ask Him what to do."

"But God doesn't talk to me!" said Tess. "I've *never* heard His voice. And I don't think He'll write, either. How will I know what He wants me to do?"

"Leave your mind open and listen," said Mrs. P. "You won't hear His answers with your ears, but you'll know He's answered you."

"How will I know," Tess asked, "if I don't hear Him talk to me?"

"Maybe somebody will have a wonderful idea and tell you," said Mrs. P. "God talks to us in His Word, and He uses others to do His work too. Remember when your friend Kara was so sick? Remember how God worked through her doctors and friends to give her love and support?"

"Yeah," said Tess. "So somebody will come and tell me what to do? And that'll be from God?"

"Maybe," said Mrs. Pilkington. "Or maybe you'll get an idea yourself. The idea will be a very good one, and it'll feel *right* deep inside of you. It'll give you peace."

"Really?"

"Really."

Tess sighed. "I sure hope you know what you're talking about, Mrs. P. No offense or anything."

Mrs. Pilkington gently squeezed Tess's hand. "Put your trust in God, Tess," she said. "You'll never be sorry."

"Okay," Tess said. "I'll try it." She gazed at Mrs. P. "Think I should talk to God now?"

"Now would be a great time," said Mrs. P., smiling.

"Okay," Tess said.

She bowed her head. "God, I'm really, really sorry about telling all those stupid lies. Now I'm in a terrible mess, but I guess You already know that, because You know everything. Anyway, Mrs. P. says You'll forgive me because You love me so much. So thank You for forgiving me. I really appreciate it, and I'll try to do better. Now I have to ask a favor. God, could You please help me get out of this jam? I don't know what to do. I'll listen for what You want me to do. Oh, and God? Could You please make the answer really *loud* or *strong* or something? I'm afraid I might not hear it otherwise. Thanks, God. Amen."

She looked up at Mrs. Pilkington. "Think that was good enough?"

"You bet," said Mrs. P.

"Good," said Tess. "I guess now I just have to wait for Him to answer me."

"Right," said Mrs. P. "It'll all work out, Tess."

Tess sighed heavily. "I sure hope so, Mrs. P. I sure do hope so!"

4

Tess Fesses Up

Tess lay on her bed, staring at the ceiling. The room was very quiet. Ashley was talking to Brian on the telephone downstairs. Her mom and Aunt Claire were washing the supper dishes.

"I'm listening, God," Tess whispered. "Whenever You want to tell me what to do, just say it, okay? I need an answer pretty fast."

She closed her eyes and listened.

She didn't hear God's voice. She wished, just once, she could hear God speak to her. She thought His voice would probably be very strong and low, but also gentle.

But Mrs. P. had said Tess wouldn't hear His voice with her ears. Mrs. P. had said she would get a very good idea either by herself

38

or from someone else. And it would just feel right. And it would give her peace.

But so far she hadn't gotten any great ideas. And she didn't feel peaceful at all!

Her thoughts shifted to Aunt Claire. How would her aunt react tomorrow when all the kids started asking her questions about Hollywood? Would she think Tess was horrible for lying about her? Would she still love Tess?

Tess thought about that, and then she smiled a little. Of course Aunt Claire would still love her! She might get pretty mad at Tess, but she would still love her.

It was just what Mrs. P. had said about Ben. Sometimes Ben was angry with Tess, but he still liked her. And maybe Mrs. P. was right. Maybe he even kind of *loved* her. After all, they were best friends!

Aunt Claire would forgive her, Tess was almost sure of that. The thought made Tess feel better.

In fact, Tess thought, maybe Aunt Claire could help her figure out what to do. Maybe Tess should warn Aunt Claire about tomorrow.

The thought of telling Aunt Claire about

her lies made Tess feel nervous. Her aunt would probably be very disappointed in her.

But Tess was sure that tomorrow would be easier if Aunt Claire knew what was going to happen.

Yes, it was a good idea to tell Aunt Claire. *Hey*, Tess thought. *I had a good idea!*

Had the idea come from God? She didn't know for sure. But it *was* a good idea, and it *did* feel like the right thing to do.

"If that idea came from You, God, thanks," Tess whispered.

She jumped up off the bed and ran downstairs.

Her mom and Aunt Claire were just finishing their clean-up work in the kitchen. Aunt Claire turned off the light and followed Mrs. Munro into the living room. They both collapsed onto the couch.

Tess wanted to talk to her aunt alone. She would have to think of a way to get her to come upstairs by herself.

"Aunt Claire," Tess said, "would you like to see my room?"

Just then Ashley strolled into the living

room. "*Your* room?" she said. She sat in the recliner. "It's my room, too, you know."

Tess rolled her eyes. "Yeah, Ash," she said, "how can I forget? You hog enough of the space!"

"No more than half," said Ashley. "How could I? You're constantly drawing a chalk line down the middle of the floor to separate us."

"If you didn't hog the space, I wouldn't *have* to draw the line!" Tess said.

"Girls, girls," said Mrs. Munro, putting her hands to her ears. "Enough already."

Aunt Claire jumped up. "I'd love to see your room, Tess."

"Great," said Tess. She glared at her sister. Ashley had better not follow them upstairs. She and Aunt Claire had some serious talking to do.

Tess led Aunt Claire upstairs. Ashley didn't follow them.

"Here it is," Tess said, bouncing down on her bed. "This is my bed. You'll sleep here, and I'll sleep on the couch downstairs."

"And there's the chalk line," said Aunt Claire, gazing at Tess's hardwood floor. "So this half is Ashley's and that's yours?"

"Right," said Tess. "But *you* can come to either side."

Aunt Claire nodded and grinned. "Thanks."

"Have a seat," said Tess.

Aunt Claire sat down next to her on the bed.

Suddenly, Tess felt shy. How was she going to tell Aunt Claire what happened? She wished she had practiced what she was going to say.

There was a long silence.

"Your room looks very nice, Tess," Aunt Claire said. She looked around. "Is this your stuffed-animal collection?" She picked up a fat lion sitting among a half-dozen other furry creatures.

"Yeah," Tess said. "That's Henry."

"Hello, Henry," her aunt said.

There was another long silence. Tess shifted on the bed. She just couldn't find the words to tell her aunt about the lies!

"Your mom tells me some of your friends are coming over tomorrow," said Aunt Claire finally.

It was now or never! Tess gulped. "Uh,

yeah," she said. "Four of my friends are coming, I guess."

"I'm looking forward to meeting them," her aunt said.

"They're looking forward to meeting you," Tess said. *Boy, were they!*

Tess took a deep breath and let it go. Here goes, she thought.

"They want to meet you—because—because—" How was she going to say it? She stared at the floor.

"Why, Tess?" Aunt Claire looked at her.

"I told them you're a great director," Tess blurted out.

Aunt Claire smiled. "Well, thank you, Tess."

Tess clasped her hands together so they wouldn't shake. "I mean, I told them that you live in L.A., and that you're a great director . . ." Her voice trailed off.

Aunt Claire nodded.

Suddenly Tess looked up at her aunt. "Do you want to do something funny?" she said. "What if we play a trick on my friends and pretend that you're a famous *movie* director! Wouldn't that be great?"

Something changed in Aunt Claire's eyes. She nodded thoughtfully.

"Did you tell them I direct movies?" Aunt Claire asked gently.

Tess looked into Aunt Claire's eyes. "Yes," she whispered.

She'd said it. All at once, Tess felt a great relief. She'd actually said it! If Aunt Claire was mad, Tess knew she could handle that. It was better than feeling scared about tomorrow.

"I see." It was strange. Aunt Claire didn't seem mad at all. She looked as if she was thinking very hard.

"I'm sorry, Aunt Claire," Tess said.

"I appreciate hearing that, Tess," her aunt said. "We can get ourselves into some pretty bad scrapes when we tell lies."

"Tell me about it!" Tess said, rolling her eyes.

Aunt Claire stood up and walked slowly to Tess's window. She seemed deep in thought.

"We're going to have to think of how to handle this," she said.

Tess thought again about the girls coming tomorrow. Her stomach rolled over. Her aunt knew the truth now, and she seemed to be accepting it without anger. But how would Britt, Tam, Kara, and Angie react when they found out about the lies Tess had told them?

Tess already knew what Britt would do. She'd run around school telling everybody that Tess was a liar. The kids would laugh at Tess.

"Liar, liar, pants on fire!" they'd yell.

It was going to be awful. Horrible.

It was going to be the most embarrassing thing that had ever happened to Tess.

She sighed sadly and lay back on the bed.

God, she prayed silently, if You have any good ideas, please let us know, okay? Because if I ever needed a good idea in my life, it's now!

The Kids Meet Aunt Claire

Tess hardly heard a word her teacher said the next day. She kept thinking about the girls coming over to meet Aunt Claire after school.

She worried and worried.

Kara and Angie had told Britt and Tam that they were invited too. The four girls were very excited. They followed Tess around school all day.

The girls sat together at lunch.

Britt asked, "Do you think your aunt will give us a list of all the movie stars she knows?"

"Will she give me her autograph?" Tam wanted to know.

"Maybe she'll have a picture of her mansion!" Angie said.

"Maybe she'll invite us to visit her if we're ever in L.A.!" said Kara.

"We could watch her direct a movie!" gushed Britt.

"And meet the *Hollywood stars!*" cried Angie.

The girls squealed with excitement.

Tess sighed deeply over her spaghetti. "I still need a good idea," she whispered to God. "Please help me."

But she didn't get any good ideas.

When everyone else in class was reading, Tess stared out the window. She thought about pretending to get sick so she'd have to go home early. (Actually, she wouldn't have to pretend very much. She felt sick to her stomach every time she thought of Britt telling everyone about her lies.)

But she decided that pretending to be sick would only put off their meeting with Aunt Claire. Her aunt was staying for a week, and Tess couldn't very well fake an illness that long.

Besides, faking was another way of lying, wasn't it? Not quite as bad as the whoppers she'd told about her aunt. But it would still be a lie.

She was sure God had forgiven her past lies. She wanted to show Him she was grateful by not lying anymore.

The day wore on endlessly, it seemed. Finally the bell rang, ending the school day.

Ben, who usually walked home with Tess, stopped at her locker.

"Ready to go?" he asked. "Roger's mom picked him up. He had to go to the dentist, so we'll walk by ourselves."

"Uh, well, some kids are coming home with me," Tess said.

"Who?"

"Kara, Angie, Britt, and Tam," Tess said.

"Oh, yeah?" Ben looked curious.

"They're coming to meet my Aunt Claire," Tess said gloomily.

"Your aunt?" Ben's eyes got big. "She's at your *house*?"

Tess nodded. "She came for a visit."

"Oh, boy," Ben said. He realized Tess was in trouble. "Oh, boy!"

Tess was glad he didn't say, "I *told* you not to tell those lies!"

"Yeah," she said. "I know. This is going to be horrible."

Just then, Kara and Angie, grinning with excitement, bounced over to Tess.

"This is so great!" Angie said.

"Yeah," said Kara. "You know the best thing about this, Tess?"

"What?" Tess said.

"Now Britt will *know* you didn't make up all that stuff about your aunt!" Kara said. "You'll show *her!*"

"Yeah," Tess said sadly. She looked at Ben. He looked away.

"You want to come, too, Ben?" Tess asked him.

"No," said Ben. "Thanks."

"Please?" Tess pleaded. She wished Ben would come. She needed at least *one* person there who wouldn't be mad. One person to be on her side!

Ben looked at her a moment. "Okay," he said.

He didn't sound as if he wanted to come. Tess knew he was just coming to be with her. Good old Ben, Tess thought. He really was a good friend!

Britt and Tam rushed up. "Come on!" Britt squealed. "Let's get this show on the road! I can't wait another minute!"

"I'm so excited!" Tam said, beami[ng]. She held up a small, colorful tablet. "I br[ought] my autograph book!"

"Good," Tess said, trying to soun[d] happy. "I'm sure Aunt Claire will be happy to sign it." She glanced at Ben, who rolled his eyes.

"Come on, let's go meet my aunt," Tess said. She added silently, *and get this over with!*

The kids walked to Tess's house, taking the shortcut through the woods.

As they walked up the front sidewalk to her house, Tess's stomach rolled over and over. She didn't want to go through that front door!

Tess's mother would still be at work. She took out her key and unlocked the door.

"Come on in, everybody," she said glumly. The girls were so excited, they didn't notice how upset Tess was. They hurried inside.

Ben paused at the door and gave Tess a pat on the arm.

"Where is she?" Britt whispered. She stood just inside the front door. She turned around in a circle looking for Aunt Claire.

ιiet. It seemed empty.
o Tess wouldn't be em-
;ht help for today, but
ant to come back?
being scared. She just
er with. "Aunt Claire?"
Tess called out.

No one answered.

Tess stepped to the bottom of the stairs. "Aunt Claire, are you up there?"

"What?" a voice came from upstairs. "Oh, I'll be right down!"

The girls giggled and stared at the top of the stairs to get their first look at the "famous movie director."

All at once, Aunt Claire appeared at the top step. She was dressed in a flowing gown that reached the floor. Her hair, which she usually wore loose around her shoulders, was tied up on her head. Tess had never seen her aunt look so beautiful.

Colorful clothes were draped over Aunt Claire's arm. She swept down the stairway, talking all the way.

"Oh, how lovely to meet all of you!" she said. "I've been waiting all day for your arrival. I have a surprise for all of you!"

The kids' eyes got big. "A surprise?" they murmured.

"We're going to put on a show!" Aunt Claire exclaimed. "I'll be the director."

"What?" Tess said. "When?"

"Right now!" Aunt Claire said. "I've got the costumes, we'll rehearse, and when your mom and Ashley get here, we'll give the performance!"

"Wow!" the girls gasped.

"I've been planning this all day," said Aunt Claire, hurrying into the living room. "Let's get started." She turned to face the five girls and Ben.

"First, I want to know your names," Aunt Claire said. "Who are you?" She looked at Britt.

"I'm Britt Spector," Britt said.

Aunt Claire stepped back and looked at Britt. "I like your long, pretty hair. Here," she said, handing Britt a long skirt and peasant blouse. "You'll be Cinderella."

Britt beamed and took the costume.

Aunt Claire walked to Tam. "And your name?"

"Tam Ling."

"Very good," said Aunt Claire. "You

have a lovely voice and a pretty smile. You'll be the singing mermaid."

She handed Tam her costume. Tam squealed, "I have fins!"

"And what is your name?" Aunt Claire asked Kara.

"Kara LaMasters."

"Good," Aunt Claire said. "You have the look of a leader. You can be Peter Pan."

Kara beamed. She took the green costume Aunt Claire handed her.

"And you?" Aunt Claire said to Angie.

"Angie Clymer."

"Angie," Aunt Claire said, "you have a sweet, pretty face. You can be Beauty."

"Can I be the Beast?" Tess said, stepping forward.

"I was just about to suggest that," said Aunt Claire, winking at Tess. "We'll have to mess you up a lot." She handed the girls their costumes.

"And you, young man?" Aunt Claire said to Ben.

"I'm Ben Brophy," he said.

"You're a Prince Charming if I ever saw one," she said.

Ben's face turned bright red. He took the costume Aunt Claire offered him.

"This is a show where all these characters come to meet in the woods," Aunt Claire said. "Each one has a song and a few lines. Then they all sing a song together."

"Great!" the kids said.

Aunt Claire passed out sheets of paper to each of them.

"Here are your song lyrics," she said. "The words of the songs go with tunes you already know, such as 'Three Blind Mice.' Go and learn your songs. Meet me here at the piano in 15 minutes."

The kids scattered to different parts of the house.

The kids practiced their songs by themselves. Then they sang while Aunt Claire played the piano. After that, they rehearsed the song they'd sing together at the end of the show.

By the time Mrs. Munro and Ashley arrived home, they were ready.

"Put on your costumes, everyone!" called Aunt Claire. "Showtime is in five minutes!"

The kids scurried away to put on their costumes.

Then it was time for the show to begin!

Mrs. Munro and Ashley sat on the living room couch. Aunt Claire stood before them.

"Ladies and . . . and ladies," she said. "Welcome to the Munro Theater's afternoon show. We've been working hard, and you're in for a treat. So sit back and relax. And let the show begin!"

And it did. The kids performed their lines and sang the songs. It was so exciting! They had all been in programs at school and church, but this was the best show they had ever been in!

When the show was over, Mrs. Munro and Ashley clapped and clapped. Tess, Ben, Kara, Angie, Britt, and Tam took their bows and grinned.

"This was a wonderful idea!" said Mrs. Munro, hopping up off the couch. "You all did a terrific job!"

"Yeah," said Ashley, grinning. "It was really good. What happened to you guys, anyway?"

"We had a great director!" the kids called out all at once. Aunt Claire looked very pleased.

Mrs. Munro left to start dinner. The girls

and Ben changed from their costumes and got ready to leave.

"Thanks a lot!" Tam exclaimed to Aunt Claire. "We had a wonderful time!"

"Yeah!" said Britt. "It was great to work with you!"

"It was my pleasure," said Aunt Claire. "And how nice to meet all of you. Now, if you will excuse me, I must help Tess's mom get supper ready. Good-bye, everyone!"

The girls called out their good-byes to Aunt Claire.

"You sure have a talented aunt," Kara said to Tess.

"She is great!" said Angie.

"Yeah, she is," said Tess. "See you guys at school tomorrow."

The girls left. Even after Tess closed the door, she could hear them chattering as they trooped down the front walk.

Tess turned to face Ben. He grinned at her.

"Your aunt saved the day," he said.

It was only then that Tess realized it. Not one of the girls had asked Aunt Claire about Hollywood! They didn't even get her autograph!

Aunt Claire had kept them so busy, they'd forgotten to ask their questions!

"She did all that work for me," Tess said quietly. "After I told lies about her."

Ben nodded. "Your aunt's really great."

"She sure is." Tess gazed at Ben. "Hey, thanks, Ben, for coming today."

"It was fun!" Ben said.

"But you didn't know it would be fun," Tess said. "We both thought it was going to be awful."

"What are friends for?" Ben said. "The Tree House Kids stick together. Roger would have come, too, if he hadn't gone to the dentist."

"I know," Tess said. "Thanks."

Ben left then, and Tess headed toward the kitchen. Aunt Claire walked into the dining room with a stack of plates and napkins.

"Aunt Claire," Tess said quietly, so no one else would hear. "Thank you for what you did for me."

Aunt Claire set her load down on the table. She came to Tess and gave her a big hug.

"I'm glad it worked out so well," Aunt Claire said.

"Me too!" Tess said.

"I'm also glad you told me last night what to expect," her aunt said. "Honesty is the best policy, you know."

"Yeah," Tess said. She grinned sheepishly. "I'll remember that."

"And it gave me time to think of a good idea," Aunt Claire said.

"That's right!" Tess said, her eyes wide. "*You* got a good idea!"

Aunt Claire laughed. "I'd been praying for one all night!"

Thank you, God, for Aunt Claire's good idea, said Tess silently.

"God has certainly helped me out of some sticky problems," said Aunt Claire. "And this was definitely one of them!"

Tess took hold of her aunt's hand. "I'm really sorry I told those lies about you, Aunt Claire."

"It's okay, honey," her aunt said. "It all worked out."

"Well, I really learned my lesson," said Tess. "And I guess I'd better tell them the whole story."

"Good!" said Aunt Claire, smiling.

"But one thing I told my friends *was* true," Tess said.

"What was that?"

"You are a *great* director!" Tess said. "No one would've thought that all those kids could put on such a great show! Most of them can hardly carry a tune!"

Aunt Claire laughed. Then she and Tess walked together back to the kitchen to help with supper.